SCOOBY-DOO!™
LIKE, DON'T LOOK NOW, BUT I THINK WE'VE GOT A "GHOUL-IN-ONE"!
FANGS, BUT NO FANGS!
Spotlight

visit us at www.abdopublishing.com

Reinforced library bound edition published in 2013 by Spotlight, a division of the ABDO Group, PO Box 398166, Minneapolis, MN 55439. Spotlight produces high-quality reinforced library bound editions for schools and libraries. Published by agreement with Warner Bros.-A Time Warner Company.

Printed in the United States of America, North Mankato, Minnesota.
102012
082013
♻ This book contains at least 10% recycled materials.

Library of Congress Cataloging-in-Publication Data

Fisch, Sholly.
 Scooby-Doo in Fangs, but no fangs! / writer, Sholly Fisch ; artist, Vincent DePorter. -- Reinforced library bound edition.
    pages cm. -- (Scooby-Doo graphic novels)
 ISBN 978-1-61479-051-8
 1. Graphic novels. I. DePorter, Vince, illustrator. II. Scooby-Doo (Television program) III. Title. IV. Title: Fangs, but no fangs!
 PZ7.7.F57Sb 2013
 741.5'973--dc23
                    2012033325

All Spotlight books are reinforced library bindings
and manufactured in the United States of America.

SCOOBY-DOO!

Table of Contents

HOW DOES FRED KNOW THE VAMPIRE'S A *FAKE?* SEE IF *YOU* CAN SPOT THE TELLTALE CLUE. THEN CHECK YOUR ANSWER AT THE END OF THIS ISSUE!

TO BE CONTINUED!

Velma's Monsters of the World:
ANIWYE

John Rozum - writer   Karen Matchette - artist
Heroic Age - colors   Sal Cipriano - letterer
Harvey Richards - editor

EWW! WHAT'S THAT AWFUL SMELL?

ONE OF OUR TWO CHOW-HOUNDS MESSED WITH A SKUNK AND GOT HIMSELF SPRAYED.

YOU MEAN SCOOBY-DOO.

REE? RUH-UH.

NO, ME.

SHAGGY, WHAT WERE YOU THINKING?

I COULDN'T HELP MYSELF. SKUNKS ARE SO CUTE. I DIDN'T THINK IT WOULD ACTUALLY SPRAY ME.

JUST BE GLAD IT WAS A NORMAL SKUNK AND NOT ANIWYE.

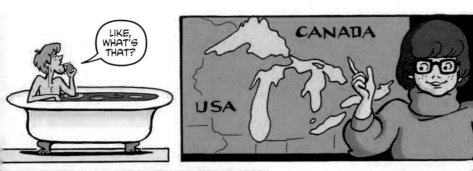

LIKE, WHAT'S THAT?

CANADA

USA

ANIWYE IS A MONSTER IN THE FOLKLORE OF THE OJIBWA PEOPLES OF THE GREAT LAKES REGION OF THE UNITED STATES.

"ANIWYE WAS A GIANT SKUNK WHO HUNTED HUMANS. IT WOULD TRAVEL AT NIGHT IN SEARCH OF PEOPLE.

"THERE WAS NO PLACE TO HIDE THAT ANIWYE COULDN'T FIND YOU. IF IT HEARD THE SOUND OF HUMAN VOICES, IT WOULD SNEAK UP TO THE SPEAKERS AND SPRAY THEM WITH ITS STINK, WHICH WAS SO POTENT, IT WOULD KILL ANYTHING IT HIT."

OoOooHHH...

AiIIIEEEE!

OUT OF THE WAY!

GASP! IT'S THE GHOST OF THE DUKE OF EARL!

SCOOBY'S MINI-MYSTERIES

BRUSH WITH DANGER

SHOLLY FISCH-WRITER
VINCENT DEPORTER-ARTIST
HEROIC AGE-COLORS
SAL CIPRIANO-LETTERER
HARVEY RICHARDS-EDITOR

...SO EVERYONE RAN OUT OF THE MUSEUM. WHEN WE CAME BACK, THE DUKE'S GHOST WAS GONE--

--AND SO WAS HIS PAINTING!

THAT'S TERRIBLE!

YEAH. AND THAT RAINSTORM OUTSIDE IS PRETTY TERRIBLE, TOO.

RUH-HUH!

HOW AWFUL FOR YOU.

AFTER ALL, I ONLY LOST A *PRICELESS ANTIQUE PAINTING*. BUT *YOU* JUST GOT *WET!*

THIS IS THE *OWNER* OF THE MUSEUM, *MISTER ART NOUVEAU.*

WE'RE SORRY FOR YOUR *LOSS*. BUT WASN'T THE PAINTING *INSURED?*

OF COURSE-- FOR *MILLIONS* OF DOLLARS! BUT WHO CARES ABOUT *MONEY* WHEN YOU'VE LOST A THREE-HUNDRED-YEAR-OLD WORK OF *ART?*

I CAME AS SOON AS I HEARD ABOUT THE *THEFT.* YOU SAY A *GHOST* TOOK IT?

OH, YOU WEREN'T *HERE* WHEN IT WAS STOLEN?

NO, I ARRIVED RIGHT AFTER *YOU* DID. BUT IF THERE'S ANYTHING I CAN DO TO HELP YOU *FIND* IT...

WELL, FOR *ONE* THING, YOU CAN TELL US WHERE YOU *HID* THE PAINTING--

--YOU KNOW, WHEN YOU WERE PRETENDING TO BE THE *GHOST!*

DID *YOU* SPOT DAPHNE'S CLUE? TAKE ANOTHER LOOK. THEN TURN TO THE *END* OF THIS ISSUE TO SEE IF YOU'RE *RIGHT!* TO BE CONTINUED!

TCK

RHR RHR RHR RHR

RHR RHR RHR RHR

OHHHHH..!

OH, FREDDIE--YOU... YOU *MISSED!*

THE HORROR! THE *HORROR!*

BAT BELFRY

A HOLE IN ONE

CREDITS:

Terrance Griep-Writer
Vincent Deporter-Art & Cover
Heroic Age-Colors
Sal Cipriano-Letterer
Harvey Richards-Editor

YOU'RE DISTRACTED, FRED--I CAN TELL.

YOU'VE HEARD THE SAME REPORTS I HAVE, DAPHNE! THERE'S A THIEF ON THE LOOSE, ONE WHO'S STOLEN DOZENS OF RARE PEARLS.

WANTED!

"THAT'S TRUE...BUT THE STATE POLICE HAVE ALL THE GETAWAY ROUTES LEADING OUT OF TOWN BLOCKED. AS SOON AS THE THIEF TRIES TO MAKE OFF WITH HIS STOLEN PEARLS, HE'LL BE CAUGHT."

"I KNOW, VELMA--I KNOW. I STILL FEEL LIKE I SHOULD BE DOING MORE..."

THAT SOUNDS LIKE AN EXCUSE FOR SECOND PLACE TO ME, JONES.

MR. IRON MAY AS WELL HAVE THAT TROPHY ENGRAVED FOR ME RIGHT NOW: "URSA GOLD, UNIVERSAL MINI-GOLF CHAMPION"...

NOW HOLD ONTO YOUR BUNKER, URSA! A LOT OF FANS HAVE COME FROM ALL OVER TO SEE THIS TOURNAMENT, AND I WON'T BE ENDING THINGS TOO SOON!

IS IT THE FANS YOU'RE WORRIED ABOUT, MR. IRON...OR THE PUBLICITY FOR YOUR PARK?

WHAT DIFFERENCE DOES THAT MAKE? GOLF WOLF PARK DESERVES PUBLICITY--AFTER ALL, IT'S THE PREMIER SPOOK-THEMED COURSE IN THE WORLD, FEATURING THE PLANET'S BIGGEST MINI-GOLF WINDMILL!

CH-KLAK

NOT TO MENTION, LIKE, THE GRAND CONCESSION STAND, DADDY-O. MAYBE YOU NEED TO, LIKE, LOAD UP ON CARBS, FRED--LIKE SCOOBY-DOO AND I HAVE...

ROULDN'T RURT...

AAHWOO

HEY, LOOK, GANG--BEHIND THIS HIDDEN DOOR. IT'S A...IT'S SOME KIND OF WORKSHOP!

YEAH, AND WHAT WORK...

THESE GOLF BALLS HAVE BEEN CUT IN HALF...AND HOLLOWED OUT.

I'VE HEARD OF SLICING GOLF BALLS, BUT THIS IS RIDICULOUS. IT JUST DOESN'T MAKE SENSE...

SURE, IT DOES. I THINK I SEE...

LIKE, GANGWAYYY!

GREETINGS, GANG...HOPE YOU DON'T MIND US, LIKE, PLAYING THROUGH-- WE'VE GOT A TWO-LEGGED SANDTRAP ON OUR TAILS!

RHE ROLF ROLF!

STILL YOU RRREMAIN--NOW YOU SHALL KNOW MY CLAWED AND TOOTHY VENGEANCE!

SHAGGY, SCOOBY, LOOKS LIKE IT'S TIME FOR A MONSTER TRAP...

OKAY, FRED, YOU CAN STOP HIM HERE!

CH-KLIK

NOW LET'S SEE WHO'S REALLY BEHIND THE GOLF WOLF!

JACK IRON!

WHAT'S ALL THAT RUMPUS? I'M GOING TO PRESS CHARGES OF DISTURBING A...

...DISTURBING A...

...FUTURE... CHAMPION.

JUMPIN' GOLF TEES!

WAIT A MINUTE--I DON'T DIG THAT GIG. WHY WOULD MR. IRON TRY TO RUIN HIS OWN TOURNAMENT?

HE DIDN'T, SHAGGY. I SAID, LET'S SEE WHO'S *REALLY* BEHIND THE GOLF WOLF!

IT'S...

UM-- WHO *IS* THAT...?

DOES *THIS* LOOK FAMILIAR?

IT'S...THAT'S THE PEARL THIEFNIK. BUT WHAT'S HE...?

THAT'S WHERE THE HOLLOW GOLF BALLS CAME INTO PLAY. THE PEARL THIEF WAS GOING TO DISGUISE HIMSELF AS A MINI-GOLF FAN, THEN GET PAST THE POLICE WITH THE PEARLS HIDDEN INSIDE THE HOLLOW GOLF BALLS!

THE PEARL THIEF KNEW HE WOULDN'T BE ABLE TO GET OUT OF THE CITY WITH THE PEARLS IN TOW...

...UNLESS HE DISGUISED THEM.

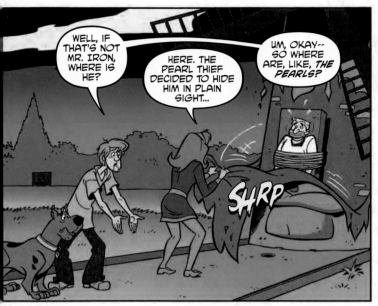

ACCORDING TO *LEGEND*, VAMPIRES DON'T LIKE *SUNLIGHT* OR *GARLIC*--AND THEY *DON'T* CAST REFLECTIONS IN MIRRORS!

BUT I NOTICED THAT *OUR* WOULD-BE "VAMPIRE" SHOWS UP JUST FINE!

ZOINKS! TWO VAMPS FOR THE PRICE OF ONE!

YEAH, YOU GOT ME. I BEEN USIN' THIS SPOOKY OLD PLACE AS MY *HIDEOUT*, SO I FIGGERED THIS *OUTFIT* WOULD SCARE AWAY ANY NOSY *VISITORS.*

UNTIL *WE* CAME ALONG! LOOKS LIKE THIS IS ONE TIME *WE* PUT THE BITE ON *YOU!*

THE END

STOP! DON'T KEEP READING! FIRST, TURN BACK AND READ THE STORY CALLED *"BRUSH WITH DANGER."* THEN COME BACK *HERE* TO CHECK YOUR ANSWER!

WHAT?! Y-YOU THINK *I* STOLE--?

YES--AND I CAN *PROVE* IT! YOU SAID YOU ARRIVED *AFTER* WE DID. BUT WE GOT *SOAKED* IN THE RAIN.

YOUR CLOTHES AREN'T EVEN *DAMP!* EVEN YOUR SHOES ARE DRY! SO YOU MUST BE LYING!

‡SIGH‡ ALL RIGHT, YOU GOT ME. I THOUGHT THAT IF I *STOLE* MY OWN PAINTING, I COULD HAVE THE PAINTING AND THE *INSURANCE MONEY*, TOO.

NO *INSURANCE MONEY*, I'M AFRAID. BUT YOU *WILL* GET FREE ROOM AND BOARD--IN *JAIL!*

THE END

SCOOBY DOO-WRITER VINCENT DEPORTER-ARTIST HEROIC AGE-COLORS SAL CIPRIANO-LETTERER HARVEY RICHARDS-EDITOR